Tam and Sam in the Orange Grove

By Jeannine Duch

Illustrated by David Sheldon

Target Skill Consonant *Ss*/s/
High-Frequency Words *have, is*

PEARSON
Scott Foresman

Sam is at the tree.

Tam is at the tree.

6

I have six bugs.

1  

One bug is silly.

I have a butterfly.

The butterfly is little.

 6 

Sam sings to six bugs.

Tam sings to the butterfly.